My left arm below the elbow does not hurt. Neither does the center of my face. Everything else does.

The other team scores. I sit and stare.

As the celebration dies down at the other end, the goalie skates in a leisurely fashion over to a black object I now notice in the face-off circle to the right of his goal. It looks like a road-kill crow. But in a couple of seconds I recognize it as my own right glove.

Ten feet beyond it lies my stick.

WOODSIE

BRUCE BROOKS

A LAURA GERINGER BOOK

HarperTrophy®
A Division of HarperCollinsPublishers

To Ryan, Randy, Colin, Chris, Moose,
Nate, 'Nother Colin, Kyle, Brian, Andrew,
Brendan, Mickey, Robbie, Matt, Jason,
Brooksie, and, above all, to Eric Lewis.

Harper Trophy® is a registered trademark of
HarperCollins Publishers Inc.

Woodsie

Library of Congress Cataloging-in-Publication Data
Brooks, Bruce.
   Woodsie / by Bruce Brooks.
     p.   cm. — (The Wolfbay Wings ; #1)
   "A Laura Geringer book."
   Summary: At the start of the new ice hockey season,
Woodsie alone believes that his teammates can pick themselves
up after several key players defect to a rival team.
   ISBN 0-06-440597-4 (pbk.) — ISBN 0-06-027349-6 (lib. bdg.)
   [1. Hockey—Fiction.   2. Teamwork (Sports)—Fiction.]   I. Title.
II. Series: Brooks, Bruce.   Wolfbay Wings ; #1
PZ7.B7913Wo   1997   97-2048
[Fic]—dc21   CIP
                                                          AC

Typography by Steve Scott
1   2   3   4   5   6   7   8   9   10
❖
First Edition
Visit us on the World Wide Web!
http://www.harperchildrens.com

Trying Out

Pumping my way down the ice, chasing the puck, faster than I've ever moved outside a motor vehicle, it occurs to me maybe I ought to kind of look up and see where I'm going. When I do, I see the pipes. The goalie with his black pads and shiny black mask is standing hunched and tense and mean, but around him, like a frame of fury, are these red pipes. Iron pipes, tough as old trailer hitches.

I hurl myself after the skittering puck, because I'm on an official breakaway and that's what I've seen guys on breakaways do. They punch the puck up ice and tear off after it, hunching their heads down, dropping their butts low, pumping their arms, launching themselves through these long powerful leg strides, skate blades making cool sounds, *sschwunch*, *sschwunch*, as they zip along. I do the best imitation I can of this, though my butt feels like it's sticking up like a whale's tail and my skates are making a sound that's more like *pss pss*. I keep after the puck across blue line, red line, and the other blue line, head down, wild with the quest for pure speed.

Behind me—closer and closer—I hear them, *sschwunch, sschwunch*. Five guys with big sticks. A *lot* of blades back there.

Crossing the line at the top of the face-off circle, I look up (and see the pipes). I pull the puck back and carry it on my forehand now, eyes on the goalie. The right phrase occurs to me. I am *bearing down on the net*. Because that's what guys on breakaways always do.

But what do they do next? That is, *before* they swerve to the side of the cage with both arms in the air to be mobbed by their grinning teammates, as the puck drops from the twine behind a goalie squirming on his back like a flipped beetle? I am missing something between the bearing-down and the celebrating. Something like a breathtaking fake or two, and then a nasty tricky shot. At this moment the goalie seems a long way from the helpless-beetle bit: He is beaming haughty death-rays at me out of his mask, and I can see that he is smiling. He gives his twenty-four-pound sharply angled stick a little twitch in my direction as I hurtle on. Behind him, in case I get past the stick, are those pipes.

I stop moving my skates for no more than one second, for a quick thought about what I might do next.

Well—one nice thing about hockey is this: If you don't know what to do next, hesitate for one second, and someone else will decide for you.

In this case, the first defenseman chasing me, Number 8—I have heard the others call him Barry— decides that I should lose my balance and lurch to the right. So, with his stick blade, from behind me, he taps my right heel forward. I lurch. By now he is even with me. Throwing up a very fine spray of ice crystals (sound: *ssshkaa*) that I feel on my face like a cold blush, he slows and rotates so that his back is to my chest. He snaps his hips backward into my gut and deftly slings his right arm over mine, trapping my right hand (which holds my stick weakly in the air like an umbrella) tight in his armpit. My butt flies up, my skates splay back to both sides, my head tries to roll off my left shoulder like an orange off a table. But I manage to watch as Barry—still clamping his right arm over mine, manipulating his stick with only his left hand—neatly sweeps the puck out of harm's way to the half boards as he rotates.

Then my back suddenly hits the back boards, Barry's number 8 fills my face mask, and the air leaves my lungs as if something in there scared it. Half a second later Barry pulls away (to accelerate after his left wing, who has snatched the puck and is speeding up ice). I slide down the boards like drool on a baby's chin, and find myself sitting with my legs straight out.

Barry never looks back.

My left arm below the elbow does not hurt. Neither does the center of my face. Everything else does.

I sit. I watch the goalie a few feet away. He is skating lightly back and forth as he keeps his eye on the action down at the other end (it seems *far* away to me, as if the players were in Europe, at least). His team scores; I hear distant cheers from somewhere between Bulgaria and the Czech Republic. The goalie gives a mildly satisfied grunt (goalies are too cool to cheer), and looks briefly over his shoulder at me. I sit and stare.

As the celebration dies down at the other end, the goalie skates in a leisurely fashion over to a black object I now notice in the face-off circle to the right of his goal. It looks like a road-kill crow. But in a couple of seconds I recognize it as my own right glove, squeezed off as my hand slipped back through Barry's armpit. Ten feet beyond it lies my stick.

The goalie glides up to the glove. Tenderly, he scoots his stick blade under it and, with a gentle flip, he lofts it over the far glass into the dark behind the penalty box. Then he turns, skates back to his crease, stops in a spray, and looks over the top of the cage at me.

He grins inside his mask. "Hi," he says. "Welcome to the wonderful world of ice hockey. Kinda fun, isn't it?"

he Wolfbay Wings Squirt A team lost only two games last year, both of them early in the season, apparently while their goaltender got through a bad case of the flu (he played anyway). They also tied two games. The rest of their games—54 more—they won. In the high air above the Wings' rink hang fifteen banners, representing the achievements of the whole hockey club. Seven of the banners belong to last year's Squirt A's. One of them is in Swedish: The Wings won a tournament in Stockholm over Christmas vacation.

This is the team my mother in her wisdom has chosen for me. I am to try out for the Wings.

"But, Mom," I said, when she told me in her office that she had completed her research and decided on the Wings, "those guys are the best team in half the country."

"Precisely."

"I played with a bunch of them at camp. They skate backward better than I do forward. Their wrist shots, their *backhand* wrist shots, are harder than my best slapshot. They read each other's minds and pass tape to tape."

She nodded, pleased. "I am not surprised."

"Four kids scored over fifty goals last season. Not counting the one who scored eighty-eight. Three of the centers had a hundred assists. The goalie has little zeroes painted on his mask in nail polish for shutouts last year. One day I counted them. There were twenty-seven. His nickname is Cheerios." I shook my head at her. "The Wings *rule*, Mom—they were totally dominant, and almost all of them will be Squirts again this year."

"'Dominant,'" she said. "I like the sound of that, Dixon. I am happy to hear you confirm my research." She patted a clipboard full of computer-printed pages on her desk. "These boys sound like worthy colleagues."

"Worthy of each other," I said. "They're way over *my* head."

She frowned slightly. "We can't have talk like that, Dixon. If something is worth doing, it is worth doing only at the highest level."

"There's a Squirt B team in the Montrose club—"

"B team! Dixon Woods!" She shuddered.

"They play about twenty games. The A teams are part of a league that covers four states! They play sixty games a season!"

"If your fondness for hockey is as profound as you claim, you should *prefer* to play more games, yes?"

"Well," I said, "but, you know, I have this obligation called 'school' . . . "

"A person of your intellectual gifts should never pretend he cannot accept extracurricular challenges."

So it went. My mother—B.S. at Stanford, M.S. at Columbia, *another* master's at some university in Germany, then the Ph.D. from MIT; NCAA chess champion at seventeen; four books published (with Oxford University Press) by the time she was thirty-five—would not hear of my playing hockey for any other team but The Best. If I must play this sport, she would agree to allow it only if I could "assert a reasonable capability at a sufficiently elevated level of competition." Otherwise, why bother?

I had spent three weeks at camp in August, four hours per day on the ice with forty kids, all of whom were much more experienced, and much better, than I was. It had been humbling.

On the first day of hockey camp, I had been feeling pretty good about myself. True, during the various skating and stickhandling drills I had been pretty crude compared to most of the guys, but I made it around most of the cones just like them, maybe just a little more slowly. (I had spent a few hours a week ice skating for the whole previous fall and winter. I had spent many hours with a hockey stick, firing tennis balls at the side of a toolshed. This was going to work, I told myself, as I took the ice for the start of the scrimmage that was the last part of every camp day. I was going to be a hockey player, all right.

Two minutes later, as my first shift ended, I thought maybe I ought to try the piano.

Sschwunch. Pss. What was that thing whizzing by me? *Sshkaa.* Where did that guy with the blue socks go? Was *that* the puck?

I felt as if I had been dropped into the middle of another civilization, on another planet, where the natives knew everything about how their world worked, while I knew absolutely nothing.

In fact, the hockey happened around me. I could not even keep up with it enough to *watch*. I was a ghost on ice.

Last year the Wings beat teams by scores like 22–3, 19–1, 16–0. All the time.

I had no chance of becoming a Wing.

But I had to pretend there was a chance, and to try out. I could only hope that I would have time to join a B team when I was cut from the Wings. My father would have been happy to see me play B or even rec league hockey. But my father had very little say in the matter.

My parents divorced two years ago. My sister Thea and I have remained in our suburban Maryland house with my father. My mother moved to a townhouse in the city of Washington. My father does the work of raising us day-to-day, but my mother pays the bills. She is a genius scientist, a government administrator, a private consultant, and a lobbyist. She works hard and makes a ton of money. My father, who is a printer and a very nice man, also works hard but makes diddly-squat.

Because my mother pays the bills, she reserves the right to "set policy." My dad lets her have her say; sometimes he does what she says, but if it makes no sense he finds a quiet way around her in the practical day-to-day. They both love us, and each of them only wants us to do well, but they are completely different.

For some reason—probably because my playing hockey is a major budget item—my mother took it on as a research project. She performed her famous "three A's"—Amass, Assess, Assign. The Wolfbay Wings were selected as the big winners of Dixon Woods, Ruler of the Ice.

"Tryouts," my mother told me, as she put away her clipboard and signaled that I could leave her office, "are to be Open." She smiled. "See that you are there. I won't insult you by wishing you good luck."

three

Bad Guy in the Slot!"

Uh-oh. As I hear the coach shout, I realize I am puckwatching, eight feet out of position to the right of my goalie, while my right wing and defensive partner fight an opponent for the puck in the corner. I am standing straight up, my weight on the outer edges of my skate blades, my stick a foot off the ice. Maybe I could be doing more things wrong if I were holding a tennis racket and wearing a scuba tank; otherwise, I've got it all covered.

Bad Guy in the Slot, eh? I turn hastily and skate forward toward the opposing center, who is indeed right in front of my goalie, anchored in perfect hockey position: skates spread, weight on the inner edges, knees bent, stick down, eyes flicking between the action in the corner, the tardy arrival of Superdefender, and the position of the goaltender.

Drawing close, I realize I should have backskated to him, keeping my eye on the puck in the corner, wedging my backside right into his gloves with momentum, bumping him backwards. As it is, now I am coming at him with my back to the person who might pass the puck right by me to him—thus giving me a perfect view as he one-times it into the net. And instead of backing into him with some force, I must stop, facing him, swivel, and politely edge sideways into his space. I might as well say, "Excuse me, pal! Got any room in this here slot for some D?"

Without taking his eyes off the scrum in the corner or his hands off his stick, the center uses a forearm to whap my left elbow into my ribs. Because my left hand grips the top of my stick, this little gesture has the effect of making my left hand yank the stick out of my right, and point it directly in front of my left skate. A terrible position. As I watch it unfold, I can't help marveling at the simple physics of it: Hey, this guy just made me into a lever!

And, gee, the winger in the corner snaps a blind backhand pass, so here comes the puck and I can't make a play!

But I get lucky. The pass just happens to graze the heel of my wobbling stick, and the puck angles away from the poised center, between my skates. The center has already gone into a short backswing with his stick, but as the puck changes direction he hesitates. I half turn into him, getting my left skate neatly beneath the blade of his raised stick, and my left arm higher up over the shaft. Thinking "I can make a lever too, fella!" I lean on the arm, hard and quick, with most of my weight.

Thus I press my own ankle sideways onto the ice with his stick blade, and of course my whole body follows.

Scrambling to my knees, I look from ice level at the goalie's skates just as the left one darts out to make a great kick-save on a sharp shot (from my man). The puck rolls on its edge right at me, passes beneath my chin, between my hands, and—I actually dip my head and look back through my legs to follow it—hits my right knee and tumbles flat. I collapse on it.

What feels like a Roto-tiller but is really just two hockey sticks slashes rapidly at my back and legs. A whistle blows. I get up. The kid who is acting as a linesman—someone's older brother, an awe-some player for the Bantam A's—picks up the puck and moves to the face-off dot, looking at me in a puzzled manner. "You okay?" he asks.

"Change!" yells the coach.

Skating to the bench, I try to look cool. It ought to be easy: The front of my sweater and pants and socks is covered with snow. A kid skates close by me on his way out to the face-off, and says, in a kind of worried voice, "Um, nice, uh, 'D.'"

I clamber along the bench and flop down. My right wing, the one who was hustling to death in the corner—his name, I think, is Ernie—punches my thigh pad with his glove. "Hey, sometimes the best thing you can do is fall down," he says.

"It's certainly *my* finest move," I pant.

Ernie nods. "It's true you suck. But you'll be okay once you learn to, um, skate in tight."

"And stay upright."

"And, um, play the man."

"And stickhandle."

"And, um, read the passing lanes."

"And count to ten and recite the alphabet and go poo-poo in the potty," says a kid down the

bench. His name is Dooby; he was a top defenseman last year. "The *whole* alphabet, and wee-wee
too. Then you'll *really* be a hockey player!"

"A," I say. "B. C . . ."

"You're doing just *fine*," Dooby says.

I stop at C. No sense rushing these things.

t the first tryout the coach of the Wings never came. I was aware of this, looking around, kind of waiting for him to show up and take charge, but I let it go as soon we took the ice. He had coached at the hockey camp this summer, as kind of an assistant. We called him Coach Kay. He was great. I got to play for him a few times in scrimmages. Once I took the puck behind the net, froze the two defensemen facing me at the corner with a fake, and backhanded a soft pass through the legs of *both* of them onto the stick of my center, who swept it into the net. Coach Kay must have mentioned the play fifteen times in the next two weeks. He'd sling his arm out if I walked by and pull me into whatever discussion he was having, then he'd describe the whole thing to the counselor or coach or visitor or parent he was talking to. He called the pass a "double meg." I found out a meg is the passing of the puck between someone's legs. You can use it as a verb too: "He megged the guy."

Even though Coach Kay liked that one pass this summer, I didn't exactly think he would recognize me and say, "Hey, Dixon, my boy—am I happy to see *you*! Naturally, I have been saving a spot for you on my championship team! Now, what number would you like on your sweater?" I had just been looking forward to seeing him again. In intimidating situations, a guy like Coach Kay has the knack of putting you at ease. The first Wings tryout felt a lot like the first day at camp. The camp was run by this former pro named Marco Barton who also coached a Squirt A team for the Montrose club, and although Marco sure knew his hockey, Coach Kay seemed to have more appreciation of the lesser guys like me. Marco spent most of his time with the kids who were polishing the last dull spots off their game. That was probably his specialty, the AA aces, while Coach Kay's was making a big deal when a C-minus kid managed to do something kind of right.

I also kept looking for the Wings' superstars from last year. I knew who several of them were from camp. But the best five or six of them never showed at the first tryout either. I thought it was probably because the coach had told them not to bother coming—leave the ice to the people who actually have to compete for a place on the team. Maybe Coach Kay hadn't come because he was skating with these half-dozen stars somewhere. Whatever.

The man who did run the tryout was named Mr. Cooper. I had seen him at camp, too, but only as a dad, picking up his son or dropping him off. His kid Cody and I had kind of been friends for the three weeks, but that was because Cody was one of those kids everybody likes, very original and funny and natural all the time. Good hockey player, too: last year for the Wings' Mite team he scored forty-two goals, and in camp he won every single backwards skating race.

If you want to spot a player who has been brought up with the difficult fundamentals, look for the guy who skates backwards well. No kid *wants* to work on his backskating when he's starting out. But a smart dad who knows hockey will make his kid turn around and practice butt first. He might even get his kid to take pride in his back-skating. Cody was like that. Which meant his dad was pretty smart about the game.

While Mr. Cooper was setting up some cones to start the tryout, I skated by Cody and said, "Hey, Codes, nice to see your father on skates," or something like that. Cody looked over and said, "He's not my father. My name is Mulligan." He tapped the piece of tape on the front of his helmet, where we are all supposed to put our first names so the coaches can call us. On his tape the word MULLIGAN was printed in red marker.

"How come Mulligan?" I said.

"Because it sounds better than Hicklebee," he said, and skated off.

Throughout the whole practice, Mr. Cooper called him "Mulligan" or "Mullgers." He called me "Dixon," because that's what I printed on my tape. Once, after I had blocked a crossing pass in a two-on-one drill, he said "Nice play, Dixie," but only that once, probably because it sounded a little cute.

I forgot all about the missing superstars and the missing coach. There were plenty of other things to worry about.

s soon as the center gets control of the puck in front of his goalie I break up ice out of the zone as fast as I can. Something about the way the players are facing makes me think I'd better get back on D without waiting around. It just feels like a rush could come.

When I get to the red line I half swivel and look back to see what's developing behind me. I was right: Three of them are tearing up ice, the center carrying the puck ahead of the wingers, none of my teammates within three steps. Cody is the right wing.

If I had hung around they would have blazed past me and had a three-on-none. As it is, even if I manage to beat them to the other end and turn around, they'll still have a three-on-one. The thought passes on the edge of my mind as I put my head down and skate as hard as possible that there's not really any disgrace in getting beat in a three-on-one. But the thought runs away in shame and disappears.

I hear them coming behind me, still spread out. I want to stop them. I snap a glance over my left shoulder. The center with the puck has pulled within six feet of me. He appears to be shadowing me. As I watch, he shifts as if to scoot by to the right and I lose sight of him.

I half swivel and look over my right shoulder. There he is, but suddenly he veers back to the left. Getting a little panicky, I swivel that way again, turning all the way around to backskate, my stick out to block him. But as soon as I have turned, he veers once more, back to the right. I cross my skates, frantic to reverse my lateral direction, and I fall.

I get lucky again, though. Just as I go down, I jab with my stick and catch the shaft of the center's. This pulls his blade off the puck and he overskates it. He has to look down and kick it out of his skates, which just gives me time to scramble up.

I glance at my goalie. He is watching the puck carrier and trying to cheat a little to the left to cover the angle from the wing over there as well. That leaves the right wing for me.

As if reading my mind, the center flips the puck through my legs to where the right wing should be.

I swivel mightily, just in time to see Cody zipping onto the puck. As I congratulate myself on turning fast enough to face him, he taps it back between my skates again.

I hear my goalie curse as I feel something hard strike me on the butt. Then I fall and slide right into the goalie and carry us both into the net on our faces. We bump heads and end up smushed to the ice in the back of the cage, both looking down like a couple of three-year-olds who have just discovered an anthill.

"Aha," says the goalie brightly. "*Here*'s that little rascally devil. I *wondered* where it had got to." He's referring to the puck, which I now see three inches from my face mask.

"Sorry," I say.

"They shot it in off your butt, you know."

"Oh."

"It looked like you were laying a quick little turd, right into my net."

"Sorry," I say again. He starts to haul himself

back to his feet, casually putting his blocker hand on my face mask to push up.

"Don't do it again," he says. "Please. Don't ever take a dump in my goal. I must implore you. For the sake of my self-esteem. It's really important that I feel secure about no defenseman-poop in my cage. After all, I have my pride." He helps me up. I hear a good deal of laughter from up the ice. As I blush inside my mask, he leans close.

"Pride is something you may never have to worry about," he says. Then he winks and pats me on the back.

am in the middle of a math problem and a grapefruit when my father sticks his head in. I am grimacing at the time. Both the grapefruit and the math problem are bitter.

"How'd it go?" my dad says.

"Okay," I say, glancing over my shoulder. I would love to put down my pencil and talk. But I have to do the math and then write three paragraphs about how Columbus was really a mass murderer with a heart made of black glass and then read a chapter about deciduous evergreens in my geography book.

My father hangs at the door. "Skates okay?"

"Skates were great," I say. He just bought me new CCM 352 Tacks. On his own, outside the budget my mother allotted for my hockey equipment. Almost everything else—hockey pants, shoulder pads, elbow pads, shin pads, gloves, helmet—we got used, with me paying fifty per cent, as agreed. I had used skates, too, some fleabit old units I bought from a high-school kid who skates as a guard at the rink where I practiced last winter. I paid eighteen dollars for them and tried hard to ignore how terrible they were.

The Tacks cost my dad almost as much as everything else put together. They were a complete surprise. It will take him about twenty hours of overtime to make up for them.

Hovering at the door, he's not taking the hint from my I'm-so-busy-studying routine, and I know all he wants is a detail or two from my ice time. So I put my pencil down and swing around to face him. I smile. He takes a few steps into the room and leans against a bookcase.

"So?" he says.

"So," I say, stretching like a puma ready for a little mountain hunting, "so—I totally sucked."

He laughs. "Tell me."

I tell him. About knocking over four out of seven cones in the first skating drill. About fanning on a shot in the first shooting drill. About hitting my right wing in the back of the knee with a clearing pass and watching while the opposing center chipped it into my net. About always seeming to turn the wrong way as the play went by, about arriving at the right spot too late, or the wrong spot too early. About how Barry turned me around and dumped me, about having to lie on the puck, about having a shot go in off my backside.

I go through it all. I am trying to be honest and realistic. I am trying to sound a little discouraged and contrite. After all, discouragement is all I am entitled to feel, isn't it? The trouble is, as I talk about all of this horrible stuff I really have to struggle to keep from bouncing out of my chair with joy. Joy! Where did *that* come from? I don't take time to figure it out; instead, I cover it up. I frown and hang my head and labor over the humiliating bits in my tale of the tryout.

But I can't hide anything from my dad. As soon as I finish, he says, "Well—I'm glad you had so much fun."

I start to protest but he laughs.

I decide to drop the pretense. But I still don't entirely understand why I feel so cool.

My father does. "You *played hockey*," he explains.

"That's more important than *how* you played. You were out there with hockey players, skating, thinking, trying things."

"But I was so *bad*."

He shrugs. "It's a difficult sport. Nobody's much good at doing something difficult the first time he tries." He leans away from the bookcase and steps to the door. "You'll get better. Probably pretty fast."

"Not fast enough to make this team."

He stops and scratches the back of his head. "Yeah. Well. Hmm."

"Mom says it's the Best or Nothing."

He sighs. "Indeed she does. Well—your mom *can* adjust to reality. If it's very definite." He gives a quick little smile with half of his mouth. "Sometimes."

I shake my head. "But if I don't get cut soon—"

"Maybe you won't," he says.

"Won't . . . what?"

"Maybe you won't be cut from the Wings. Maybe you'll surprise yourself. Maybe you'll make the team." He raises his eyebrows. "I think today has made you want to pretty bad. And not just for your mother. Hmm?"

He's right. It's hard to face it, but he's nailed it. The fact is, after playing with those good players today, I want to be one of them. If I were to say the words "B Team" at the moment, I'm afraid I would shudder and sneer, even though I would be lucky even to make a decent "B Team," and would probably spend a great season playing hard hockey at that level. Those kids are great too.

oach Kay isn't at the second tryout. Once again it is Mr. Cooper who skates, puts down the cones, starts the drills.

The five superstars aren't there either.

Nobody else seems to think anything is wrong; all the other kids are just skating and acting normal. I don't know if this is because they haven't noticed the missing Wings, or because they know something I don't. I'm used to noticing lots of things other people don't bother about. But a head coach who doesn't show up for tryouts?

In line for the first drill I'm in front of Barry, the defenseman. He seems like a good guy, and he was a Wing last year, so I decide to ask him. Kind of casually I say, "So where's Coach Kay?"

He gives me a quick look. "Oh, hi," he says.

"Hi."

He glances around, as if to see if anyone is

listening. "You don't know?" he says.

"No."

It looks as if he sighs a little in the secrecy of his helmet. "Oh, well. Um, Coach, like, is—he's—he, like, changed clubs."

"He did what?" I squawk.

Barry holds up a hand and looks quickly over his shoulder. Mr. Cooper is back there, telling a kid something about holding his lower hand higher on the stick. Barry turns back to me. "Yeah. He left. He left to go coach at Montrose."

"You're kidding!"

For a second his eyes glare, but then they go dull. He shrugs. "Marco Barton got him to go over there. He's, like, putting together this superteam. It's no big deal." He doesn't seem to want to say anything more.

"But—"

"No, it's no big deal," says another voice. I turn and see Dooby behind me. "The big deal is, he took our five best players with him."

"Speak for yourself," Barry snaps.

Dooby rolls his eyes. "Oh, excuse me, Barry. Somehow he forgot you. So, okay—he took five of our best *six* players."

Barry is blushing. "I didn't mean me," he says.

"No?" says Dooby. "Then who *do* you mean? We lost our top three scorers and two best defensemen. The only reason he didn't steal our goalie is that he moved up to Peewees. We got *zip* left, except a bunch of second and third liners who'll spend the first half of the season wondering where all the rebounds are, and who's going to catch up to that guy pulling away with the puck toward our net." He shook his head and spat neatly through his cage. "We got total zipola."

I ought to keep my mouth shut but I don't. "It seems to me you still have some *great* players—"

"Yeah, well, no offense, man, but it *would* look that way to you, wouldn't it? But take my word for it, when Ace Defenseman Barry here spins *you* off the puck it's not quite the same as him trying to spin a hundred-fifty-pound mean winger from Philly who can actually *skate*, see?"

He doesn't say it unkindly. And I have to admit he's right. But Barry won't give in.

"We'll be all right," he says.

Dooby sighs heavily. "Yeah. Well. At least Coach

Coop is a good guy. I had him my first season in Mites. He knows as much as Coach Kay and all that. Maybe more. But let's face it—the Coach can't get out there on the ice and make the plays. We need hockey players."

"But for sure you'll still get to pick the best kids in the area," I say. "I mean, the *Wings*—"

Dooby snorts. He gestures ahead of us as a heavyset kid loses the puck in his skates, steps on it, and falls down. "Do these look like the best players in the area to *you*? No offense, but there are people here who make you look good. At least you have good hockey sense, anybody can see that, but look around—some of these guys couldn't spell PUCK if you spotted them the P and the K."

Trying not to feel *too* good about Dooby's comment on my hockey sense, I say, "But won't more people come out for the team, then?"

"When are they going to do that? This is the second of three skates. This is it. Your mighty Wolfbay Wings, Squirt division." Another kid, a skinny one this time, overskates the puck and looks down for it and runs smack into the boards. Dooby laughs, then shakes his head.

"At least the really awful people—like me, I know I'm one of the worst—won't be here."

Barry says, "Have you counted to eighteen lately?"

"What—"

"Go ahead," says Dooby, sweeping his arm at the ice.

I look around and count. Leaving out the seven brothers or cousins or whatever who are just helping out, there are sixteen kids on the ice. Why didn't I notice before how few of us there were?

"Welcome to the club, Dix," says Dooby.

"I don't—"

"You need at least sixteen or seventeen kids for a team," Barry says. "Three lines of three, three pairs of defensemen, a couple of goalies, some spare change."

"How many'd you count?" says Dooby.

"Sixteen."

He nods. "Then I'd say Coach Coop won't be facing the agonizing task of needing to let go of *any* of these finely conditioned athletes."

I hear a whistle and turn; it's my turn to go in the shooting drill. I skate. But I can barely concentrate enough to carry the puck. I can only think:

I'm going to be a Wing! In the back of head is a niggling voice trying to remind me that it's a pretty slinky way to "make" a team, but I blow the voice off. I'm going to play hockey for the Wings.

"Shoot it!" hollers the teenager running the drill.

I whack at the puck. My stick stubs it and it rolls six feet wide of the net. The goalie, the same one who shoveled my glove over the glass, drops melodramatically into an exaggerated butterfly split and swings his blocker out in the direction of the shot. "Whew!" he says. "I sure got lucky on *that* hummer!"

I can't help laughing. In fact, it's hard to stop. Skating back into line, I look up. All those banners up there, with the borrowed flying-wing logo of the Detroit Red Wings—the very wing I'll be wearing on my chest this year. Who cares about Coach Kay? Who misses the kids with sixty goals?

I'm going to be a hockey player. I'm going to be a Wolfbay Wing. I'm going to—

Cody skates by in a flash. "Balance check!" he says, and lightly hooks my right knee in passing. I twirl and fall. Another old Wing taps my stick away, then backhands it down the ice in a long pass to Dooby, who stickhandles it like a puck toward the untended goal. He wiggles his shoulders in a terrible fake one way, then the other; he winds up for a huge slapshot, then lightly slides my stick into the net.

"Whose stick is that?" hollers Coach Coop.

"Mine," I squeak.

"Give me ten push-ups," he says. "Wings don't drop their sticks. Okay?"

"Okay," I say. And actually, the push-ups don't feel so bad.

Practicing

eight

The puck is loose between the circle and the boards, and with a quick jump I decide to pinch in from the point and take it. "Cover!" I yelp, hoping the wing will drop back. I pick the puck on my forehand and swing in toward the slot. Shinny, playing center against me, slides that way to cut me off; as soon as he crosses his skates I switch to the backhand and swing outside him and behind the net. Now as I come around I look for my own center, Boot, and start to slide him a nice forehand pass—

Whistle. "Freeze!" yells Coach Coop.

It's pretty hard to "freeze" on ice skates—you tend to keep moving. But by now we know what to do, so each of us goes back a few paces to the positions we held just before I made the pass. Coach skates over to me.

"Good," he says. "Here we have Woodsie with the puck on his forehand and no defense at his heels. He's got a lot of options, right? Right, Boot?"

"No."

Laughter from a couple of kids. "No?" says the Coach.

Boot shakes his head inside his helmet. "No. When the Boot is on the ice, there's only one option: Get it to the Boot." More laughter.

"Well, of course," says the Coach. "But—excuse me for asking—where would the Boot like to receive this puck?"

Boot is in hockey position, facing me, with his right skate on the edge of the crease line. He's a left-handed shot, so he's ready for a one-timer. "Right here," he says, tapping his stick a foot from the line.

"Sure, Boot, whatever you say," says the Coach. He picks up the puck and skates over, placing it on exactly the spot Boot indicated, as if he were putting a diamond necklace on a velvet cushion. Boot grunts. As Coach backskates to where I am standing, he cuts a quick glance at Lyle, the goalie.

"Before we play it, anybody see anything wrong here? Not you, Woodsie," he says, as I raise my hand.

No one says anything.

"Is Boot going to score?"

Almost everyone nods or hollers "Yes!" or "Goal!" or "He shoots he *scores!*" Cody says nothing, I notice. He's probably seen this bit before.

"How many times out of ten is he going to put the puck in?"

"Ten!" they holler.

Coach nods. "Okay, then, we'll see. Play it!" He blows a quick toot on his whistle.

Boot was ready, with his stick already drawn back; at the signal he snaps his stick at the puck. But it is no longer there. With an even quicker, slighter motion, Lyle has flicked it away.

"Now let's try it with the pass," Coach says. "Skate to the same positions."

We reverse the movie and do it. I skate around the back of the net, see Boot, and zip him a pass. But Lyle deflects it with his stick, along the line to the corner. We do it five times, and the same thing happens every time.

"All right," Coach says when we have stopped after the fifth pass. "Let me give you a little lesson in anticipation." He grins, and looks around. "*Spatial* anticipation."

"Each of us is spatial in his own way," says Dooby.

Coach skates to Lyle and takes his stick. He lays it on the ice, angled out from the post where Lyle stands. Then he takes Boot's stick and moves to the very end of Lyle's. He leaves about eight inches of ice between the two blades and lays Boot's stick down along the same line as the goalie's. Then he takes Boot by the shoulders and guides him over to the shaft end of his own stick.

Boot is now about ten feet farther away from the goal than he was. "Well, *this* certainly sucks," he says. Everyone laughs.

The Coach addresses everybody. "If you are waiting for a pass to come to you from somewhere in *front* of the cage—from the point, the corner, the half boards—then you can plant yourself in the slot. No problem. Easy money."

He skates back to me. "*But*—if the pass is coming from behind the cage—and the goalie happens to have even a low-to-mediocre intelligence, like Lyle here—you are only going to *receive* that pass if your stick blade is out of reach of the goalie's stick blade." He turns and pushes me. "Which means the passer should swing a little wider, too." He looks around. "Okay? Everybody understand? Boot, think you can hit the net from there? Okay, let's try it."

n the way home in the car, Thea asks, "Why do you call that boy Boot?"

I hesitate. You're kind of never supposed to question a nickname, or acknowledge it even; you just accept it, and everyone else does too, even if you don't know why it was chosen ("It sounds better than Hicklebee"). But Thea doesn't know the deal with nicknames, obviously. And she's being very nice about this hockey business in the family, driving me to every practice—twice a week—and usually hanging around to watch. So I decide to answer.

"His name is Norman," I say, "which, first of all, is no name for a hockey player."

"I can see that," she says, nodding. "It's no name for any *human*."

"He goes to this rich private school where they have lots of computers. In fact, the school has a hard-drive laptop for every kid from the fourth grade up."

"Ooh, risky. Lots of Tetris in history class."

"Right. So, now, Norman isn't the kind of kid who exactly likes to follow instructions. He gets kind of impatient. Wants to just figure it out on the wing."

"Why don't they call him Birdy?"

"Come on," I say. "He's a *hockey player*. Birdy?"

"I guess not."

"Anyway, Norman gets going on his laptop well in advance of his teacher's instructions. And he crashes it."

"Ouch. Two kilos."

"They probably get a discount, but even so. The thing is, Norman realizes that even at a rich school he might get into a little trouble for crashing a two-thousand-dollar computer because he didn't want to listen to his teacher tell him how to work it. So, he swaps with another kid."

"What is this kid's IQ?"

"Well, Norman can be very convincing. The screen on his computer just keeps scrolling numbers. He sits there, nodding confidently, mumbling figures, writing things down in a notebook. The kid beside him wonders why *his* screen just keeps saying 'A> INPUT ERROR' or something. He keeps peeking over at Norman."

"'Geez, how come *his* compooter works so good?'"

"Right. Eventually he asks. And Norman says, 'Well, you just have to boot it up.' He tells the kid he has booted his own already. But since he's such a nice guy . . .'"

"Okay, I get it."

"He does it eleven times."

Thea gawks. *"Eleven?"*

I nod. "Yep. He crashes eleven hard drives. Until finally the teacher investigates why so many kids aren't getting their stuff done . . ." I raise my hands. "So he's Boot."

We drive on for a while. I tell her some of the other nicknames—Prince (a very short kid who sings all the time in falsetto instead of talking), Zip (as in zero—the goalie), Java (a fat kid who brings a thermos of coffee to the bench for every game), Feets (he has big ones and trips a lot), and others. Thea chuckles.

So do I. I feel pretty good right now, after three weeks of being a Wing. Lots of things are going right. My mother is pleased with me for making the team. (Somehow, I have neglected to mention the conditions that earned me the spot.) My father listens to every detail when I get home from practice every Tuesday and Thursday, and marvels at the lessons I am learning in hockey (though, somehow, I have neglected to tell him the lessons are so fundamental that any true A team shouldn't need them). Thea suddenly likes the hockey rink (and, I think, Cody's older brother Jerry, who helps out at most practices).

For me the best part is getting to be a member of a team. I have never been part of a group committed to doing one complicated thing all together. At school, when you "team up" for projects you don't really think that hard about each other. You don't share the work so much as divide it. You don't learn tricks from each other. You don't join up so you can stand against the rest of the world.

Joining a team, especially one that existed before you came along, takes a while. You need to watch and listen, be kind of careful. It's work, not just putting on the right sweater.

Twelve of the kids were teammates last year, on Mites or Squirts; most of them have been playing together since they were five or six years old. So this season is just another chapter, somewhere in the middle of their long book. If I'm going to work my way into the story, I have to slip into it at just the right place, in just the right way, a new guy whose appearance in the plot seems natural, even necessary.

In the meantime, everybody's being pretty decent. Two or three of the guys seem bitter about the desertion of last year's stars, and sometimes they take it out on me and the three other new players. But overall the team seems to have taken an attitude of toughness and pride. One day after practice, while the usual jive was going on in the locker room, with people throwing balls of tape and making animal noises and stealing each other's socks, Barry, who was unlacing his skates, suddenly snarled, "We don't need those jerks." He didn't look up, he didn't say any more, he didn't explain what he meant or why it was on his mind. But everybody stopped messing around for a few seconds.

The trouble is—I keep wondering if maybe we

really *do* need those jerks. Or at least a couple of them. We are proud, we are tough, we are cool and funny and loud, but I'm not sure we are a very good hockey team.

It's true that our drills and scrimmages have gotten a lot tighter very quickly. Those of us with less experience and skill seem to have really picked it up, thanks to Coach Cooper. The veteran Wings have been good, too. They don't treat us as disgusting scrubs, but they don't cut us much slack either. They don't condescend to us by being all sweet and patient when we mess up, or by congratulating us when we perform some maneuver that ought to be standard for a Wing but is a triumph for one of us. We *are* Wings; our teammates expect us to focus and make the plays. If, in order to do so, we need to learn something, then we'd better learn it *fast*.

I hope Dooby was wrong. I hope the plays we are starting to make against each other now—I had two assists today in scrimmage, and stopped a two-on-one against Cody and Prince—are plays we can also make against other good teams.

Certainly we'll get the chance to show what we've got. Earlier this week, the team and the parents voted on whether to play the season as an A team or a B team. It was unanimous: The Wings Squirt squad will be the Squirt A's again. Next, we voted on whether to play a twenty-four-game schedule against only teams in the Maryland–D.C.–Northern Virginia area, or to add another twenty-two games against teams in an elite league that covers parts of Pennsylvania, New Jersey, and New York. This will mean quite a few road trips—nights in hotels with pools and ice machines and elevators (for racing), lots of road meals at fast food places, lots of unknown faraway ice rinks, lots of adventure. There is no adventure, the veteran Wings say, in playing around here. And besides, there's this Marriott in West York with a six-story open lobby and four fountains and if you stand in the right corner you can loft paper airplanes down from the top into *every* fountain. . . .

Again, it was unanimous. We will hit the road.

In fact, we will hit it soon. Today, Coach Coop handed out our schedules. Our first three games will be on the road over one weekend, against teams in Pennsylvania. We have ten days left to get ready.

As Thea begins to talk about how extremely cool hockey sweaters would look on girls, especially the blue one with the musical note on the chest, I cannot help letting a huge swell of excitement take me over. To hide my grin I look out the window. Three games, in one weekend, a little over a week away. As I think about it, I realize Dooby *is* almost certainly wrong. We are looking *good*. We will be ready.

I relive my second assist, a blind backhand pass to Ernie at the corner of the net, with my back to the net and a defenseman chopping helplessly at my kidneys. It couldn't have been any quicker. It couldn't have been placed any better. Even Cody, who rarely pays compliments, said, "Cool pass, Woodser."

I let myself admit it: It was an "A" pass.

ten

What I think I like best about hockey," says my dad as he brings my skates to the locker room after getting them sharpened, "is the fact that no one can wear some fakey trendy sports shoes every day and play the role at school."

He says this as if he goes to school every day himself. And somehow that sounds okay. By now the guys on the team have gotten to know my dad a little, and nobody snorts when he says something that could come from a kid.

"Hmm," says Zip, looking up from his leg pads. "Maybe we're missing a major marketing opportunity."

"Skate boots without the blades," says Barry. "You can buy them that way."

"But you can't walk in them," says Coach Coop, as he tightens Cody's skates. "They're too stiff."

"A certain type of historically verified hockey

footwear suitable for everyday use is readily attainable," says Shinny, in his usual style. He is fully dressed. He is always fully dressed. Looking at him, I realize I cannot recall seeing him put his stuff on in the locker room. Maybe he comes from home suited up. Maybe he *lives* suited up.

"You must be referring to the crude sandals worn by early hockey players back in the Esophagus Era," says Dooby.

"Yeah, the kind with the pieces of used truck tires for soles," says Java. "The kind they keep finding when they unearth those primitive ice rinks in Egypt."

Shinny waits, unfazed, to continue his lecture. "For many generations, children playing first shinny and then hockey in more temperate areas of Canada, unable to find playable ice, convened their games on areas paved with cement. To imitate the sliding mobility so fundamental to the feeling of the game, these resourceful young athletes adopted the practice of wearing loose gum rubber boots, several sizes too large. Worn unfastened, these floppy integuments allowed a good deal of slipping and sliding."

"Thank you, Shinny," says Coach Cooper. "That was enlightening."

"But what it means," whines Boot, "is that the most I can hope for when I grow up is an endorsement contract for a bunch of oversized rubber galoshes."

"The Boot Boot," I say.

"There's probably *dozens* of dollars in such a product," says Cody.

"As a style item, it *does* sound about right," says my dad. "Plain old scuffy ten-buck boots for hockey players, hundred-sixty-dollar six-color sneakers with flashing lights for all the other wanna-be's."

Dooby snaps on his helmet and stands up. "Until the ten-buck boot look gets 'cool,'" he says. "Then we drop it."

eleven

t one point just before the scrimmage a buzz seems to whip between some of the players on the ice, followed by a grim silence. All of a sudden, it's tense out here. I feel it, but I don't get it. Seeing a couple of heads turn quickly toward one corner and quickly back, I look.

There are two kids in blue letter jackets with yellow sleeves leaning against the boards on the other side of the glass, watching us. I can't see their faces through the thick glass. But I think I recognize one of them from hockey camp. His name is Peter. He was one of the Wings' big scorers last year.

One of the guys who left. To play for Marco on the Montrose club. Whose colors are blue and yellow.

A deserter.

I look at Barry. His mouth is clamped tight behind his face cage. I look at Dooby and Zip.

Dooby is skating in little circles while he waits for the scrimmage to resume, and I hear him whistling. Zip waves his catching glove at the boys. Peter waves back. As he does, Zip turns his back, sticks out his butt, grunts loudly, and pretends to catch something in his glove.

Behind all of this I hear Prince's falsetto. He is singing an old soul song the P.A. plays sometimes at breaks in the Capitals' games:

You broke my heart cuz I couldn' dance
You didn' even want me around
But now I'm back to let you know
I can really put 'em down

Cody begins to dance beside him.

"All right," says Coach Cooper. Even he sounds tense. "Let's play some hockey." He gives a quick glance at the corner, then drops the puck between Cody and Prince.

As soon as it hits the ice, I know this scrimmage is going to be different. Prince jams his shoulder into Cody's face and jabs his stick at the puck, hard; Cody ignores the puck but hooks his blade behind

Prince's left knee and yanks, also hard. Prince goes down, holding Cody's stick. Cody kicks the puck back toward me, then swats Prince in the helmet with his glove as he pulls on his stick. Prince lets go, but slashes Cody across the knees as he skates away. And this is *supposed* to be a non-checking level of hockey for another month.

Suddenly everyone is in motion—wheeling or dashing or sprinting, tapping the ice for a pass, slashing at the other guy's speedy legs. It is as if the whole ice surface lights up from below with a cold, fierce glow. I watch for only an instant, but that is too long: Java plucks the puck off my stick at full speed, and gives me a hard, glancing hip at the knee for good measure. Surprising myself, as I spin I hook his right elbow with my stick. It slows him a little, and Barry barrels into him low from the other side, flips him onto his tailbone, and slaps the puck up to me. I half swivel, feeling someone coming from behind, and backhand a pass toward Cody along the left boards. A tenth of a second after I release it, I am leveled. Picking myself up, I throw a shoulder at a passing red jersey, knock somebody down, see the puck skittling by, slap at it in the general direction of the cage, feel a stick pull on my ankle, go down hard on my elbows, hear a shout, scramble up, looking for somebody to shove or bump, and find three or four gloves swatting me in the face cage, on the helmet, in the chest.

"Great pass," voices say. "Good hit." "Nice look."

Pass? Hit? Look?

Well, yes. It appears that I disrupted a three-on-two with a check, intercepted a pass to the headman, put the puck on the tape of my racing left wing, sending him in on a breakaway that he duly buried. "Way to step up, Woodsie," says Coach Coop, "way to think the play." Think? To me the "play" felt like high-speed chaos. I made no real choices; I had no thoughts. I reacted like a dog that finds himself in traffic.

I made a great play.

Then the puck drops and it all starts again. Hits, spins, falls, curses and hoots and grunts, but most of all speed, energy. Is this hockey? This time I begin to see things a little longer, I recognize a thought or two, I find myself backskating against a rush and realize that is what I am supposed to do so I must have decided to do it, but I never felt the thought. Then I have poked the puck to the corner, chased it, turned my back into the other guy racing with me, flipped it up the boards out of the zone right into the path of Cody swooping by into the attack zone.

It is a perfect pass. But did I *do* it? It seems as if it just *happened.* But there is no time to think, here comes another rush, but this time I go for a shoulder deke and fall down and get up and . . .

The whole scrimmage goes this way. People smash into me. I crush people. Sticks hit my pants with a thud, my helmet with a clack, sounds I hear seconds after they are made because I am always heading for the next thing. Excitement pops and cracks and booms through us all, second after second, always building like the noise of a fighter plane zooming to the sound barrier. No stopping the frantic rush of it all; even at the whistles we just pause, tense and hot, ready to pounce. I completely lose my sense of time. One moment erases the previous one.

And then there is a rush that peters out, a fallen defenseman who does not spring back up, a puck that skitters to the corner and is watched rather than pursued—and suddenly we all sag, exhausted.

It is over. In acknowledgment Coach Coop blows his whistle. We all lean over, stick across knees, sucking air.

"Good effort," Coach says. "Get some water." He too is panting.

Upright, getting stiff already, we turn toward the gate at the corner. Halfway there, someone remembers, and turns his head back to look. The other heads turn too.

The two boys are watching, just as before, their faces blanked by the glass.

Zip, beside me, hollers, "Knock knock!"

We can't hear the response, but it looks like Peter's mouth moves. *Who's there?* we all imagine. Zip hollers, "Howard!"

Again Peter's mouth moves, and in our heads we all say it: *Howard who?*

Zip pulls off his helmet and juts his face out. "Howard *you* like to kiss my—"

"That's good, Zipper," says Coach Coop, skating up behind us. We turn and glance at him. He's smiling.

When we turn back to look at the far corner, the blank faces have gone.

twelve

My mother has decided not to accompany me on the road trip; there is a conference of geologists in Georgetown at which she needs to "show a presence." Although I am really grateful for the way she has supported me in all of this hockey stuff, and although I am eager to play for her and let her see how her research and investment have paid off with the Wings, I am relieved she decided not to come to the first games. For one thing, I may not play all that much; Coach Cooper seems to feel we should all get equal time on the ice, but in the crunch of a close league game he might change his mind, double-shift his good players more, let the rookies watch. For another, if I do play, I might be a little nervous and spazzy. And finally, I'm afraid my mom is not the kind of person who would smile and shake her head tolerantly as sixteen boys ran up and down the corridors of a hotel throwing ice and playing tag on stairwells and flying paper planes down through lobbies into fountains.

My father, whom my mom designated to stand in for her, can be as immature as any ten-year-old. He would probably be right there with us hanging over the sixth-floor parapet, a paper jet in each hand. But in fact he cannot take me either. The late fall is a very busy time in his print shop and he will probably be working seven days a week for the next two months. A weekend off is impossible.

This seems to be a common problem, though. In the locker room after the most recent practice, Coach Cooper asked each kid how he was getting to Pennsylvania, and handed out a list of parents willing to pile the riders into their vans. He made a point of talking to my dad himself, and offered to take me with him and Cody. I'm happy with this. I hope we talk hockey all the way up.

The last couple of practices have been much like the scrimmage we put on in front of Peter and his Montrose friend when they "spied" on us last week. Intense. We want to keep that edgy feeling. Even when Cody and Zip and Dooby launch a new weirdo comedy routine while we dress before every skate, none of us join in *completely* the way we used to. We all keep part of our minds on hockey.

Coach Cooper seems kind of excited, too. He speeded us along through his individual-fundamental stuff and started putting us to work on team-strategy stuff in the last two sessions. It's not exactly advanced, but it does involve faster thinking, and it's based on the idea that we can read what's going on in front of us on the ice and decide how to react. We worked on several variants of the breakout play, tying each to a particular attack that carries through the neutral zone into the other team's end; we worked on a rotation of forwards and the defenseman along one side of the offensive zone, to set up a pass from the point to the weak-side winger coming out from behind the net; we worked on a three-man trap on the puck carrier as he comes out of his zone and approaches the red line. Everyone loved it, except Boot, who just wants to float until the puck pops out and then shoot it from wherever he is, and Shinny, who was annoyed that the background on the trap play couldn't be located in his memory of break-throughs in the history of strategy and tactics.

At each practice we also get other things—a roster listing players' birthdays and addresses, a set of road maps showing the places we will travel, a calendar with the games written on it, a form for ordering Wings' caps and shirts and jackets. My teammates barely notice these papers; most stuff them into a pocket of their equipment bags alongside their damp socks or sweaters, while some just leave them on the floor of the locker room.

Their indifference amazes me, though I say nothing. The lists and maps and forms are the most fascinating pieces of paper I have ever owned. They reveal so much, and they imply even more. I keep them to myself for days, take them out when I am supposed to be doing homework, spread them on the blue blanket of my bed, study them. To me, these are the certificates of hockey membership, registrations of hockey reality, indications of hockey possibilities. Yes, of course, I say to myself, it just *figures* that Prince was born on June 2 and Barry on November 27—somehow these dates are just right.

And I am one of them. When I come to my own birthday as I go down the list, I think about it the same way I do the others. It's hard to explain how much this means to me, or why. It's not what I am used to. In every "group" at schools or churches or clubs, I never quite slip into the mix. Either no one accepts me quite all the way, or I never accept the group. It always seems "they" are a lot more like each other than I am like "them."

Now I was just one kid on a team. Not just any team, either—a *hockey* team. That's what made the difference. Hockey is the best sport for being equal. For working together. For supporting each other. That's one reason it is the only sport I have ever wanted to play. On soccer or baseball or football teams, there are starting players, then subs who play a little, and lastly scrubs who don't play at all. But on a hockey team, five people skate a one–two minute shift, then get off the ice so the next group can skate one–two minutes, and so on, right through everyone. Only the goalie plays all the time; the other players share the ice time pretty equally.

The reason is simple: The game works best played at top speed without any effort held back. But if you give it everything you have, you wear out fast. So, go ahead—wear yourself out! Then you can come off the ice, recover for a few minutes while your teammates wear themselves out, and go back out to skate another full-speed shift.

Hockey is the only sport I know where you get to see everyone pushing himself to the limit every moment of the game: offense, defense, transition, the whole range. This makes for a different team feeling. When your teammate skates to the bench with his tongue hanging out, you aren't going to skate out and take his place and give about seventy-five per cent. No way. Every player respects the effort of the guy in front of him. So every shift, you get one hundred percent, one hundred percent, one hundred percent.

But even then hockey is different. In baseball, if you are *willing* to give one hundred percent—and most baseball players are; I respect the kids I know who play baseball—you still don't really *get* to. What can you do? You have to stand around a lot. You watch, you think, you wait in position, and you pounce if you're lucky enough to get the ball hit near you.

In hockey, nobody stands still for an instant.

Even when you are "waiting" in position you are moving fast on your skates. There is always someone to check, with or without the puck; that someone is usually moving fast. There is always a screen to set in front of the goalie—skating by him at the very second a teammate takes a shot from farther out, so the goalie doesn't see the puck coming—or an opponent's screen to break up. When the puck is loose it moves fast and very weirdly, and as you try to control it to make a play, there are all these sticks jabbing at it and arms grabbing at you and elbows whamming at you, and fighting all of that off takes a lot of energy. But you would gladly spend every flicker of energy left, just to spoon that puck away and snap a pass to a teammate dashing up toward open ice. You would gladly lie down and die one second later, if that's how much you had to give. It sounds stupid, but that's how you feel if you play hockey. Hockey is for hard work, not glory. Only your teammates understand.

It is great to have teammates at last. It is great, at last, to get to work.

thirteen

Billy beats me to the high slot and here comes the puck from Prince on the wing. Zip is out to cut the angle in case Prince shoots. He doesn't. It's an excellent pass. All Billy needs to do is put his stick on the ice; the puck will deflect right into the net. It's so simple it makes me sick. Still I chase him down. Maybe I can make it a little complicated.

Billy is set, skates wide, cruising slowly in pace with the pass, backside out to keep me off, stick down, eye on the puck. Instead of taking the shortest path to him, which would leave me nothing to do but cross-check him for a penalty or perch politely on his butt, I swing wide to his stick side. I lean severely toward him, lifting my outside skate, cutting a huge spray with the inside of my left *(ssschonk)*, and for a second I am poised there exactly between going forward (out of control) or going down (also out of control). For that single second, however, I am completely still, just where I want to be, and completely in control.

I use the moment to jack Billy's stick off the ice with my own. The next instant I am plummeting down, and I can watch as the puck passes undisturbed beneath Billy's raised blade and past my upraised skates to the corner. Then I hit the ice with a body-slam.

Billy cusses—he's the youngest kid on the team and he thinks cussing makes up for it—and takes a moment to slash my helmet before he goes after the puck. That's fine with me. Cussing takes energy, slashing takes time. I get control of my arms enough that when Billy does decide to zip to the corner one of my gloves just happens to knock his inside skate off line just as he puts his weight on it. He doesn't go down (which is good) but he swerves (which is also good). Recovering his line to the puck takes another half-second, and by then Dooby has skated into the play.

Reaching with one hand on his stick, he taps the puck back toward Billy just as Billy arrives full speed. It goes right between his skates and comes medium-fast toward me.

I have gotten back to my knees facing the play, off the right post. I hear skates behind me, so I have no time to scramble the rest of the way to my feet. I hoist my stick and slide my hands down, right hand all the way to the heel, left hand two feet higher, and I sweep at the puck backhand. With my hands so low I get unbelievable leverage. The puck whips over the blue line six feet off the ice—Cody is cruising in on the attack and jumps straight up but it's over his upstretched hand—and falls back out there somewhere in the neutral zone.

Billy gives me another slash and cuss as he goes by.

The whistle blows. "Take a seat in the sin bin, Bill," says Coach Cooper. "Got to control that temper. Good play, Woodsie."

"Nice rush," I tell Billy as he cusses his way to the penalty box. "Way to finish."

Is it really me who says that?

hen you put ten skaters on a sheet of ice and they all want the same thing, you don't get ten people going after it on the same path, at the same speed, with the same angle, following the same strategy. You get ten completely different people, each trying eight things every twenty seconds, moving behind, beside, in front of, and through each other, fast, and in all directions.

Skating through a hockey shift is like trying to run through a forest in which the trees are all falling.

There is something inside you, probably in your brain, some automatic talent, that always kicks in and struggles to *set* you, to let you know just where you are, which way is which, how your movement fits in with the movements of things around you. This is a very smart part of your brain. It makes you feel okay in all kinds of situations when you could panic and go nuts—when you are knocked over by a wave in the ocean and tumbled under the water with the currents pulling all ways at once, for example. It is almost impossible to fool this here-you-are talent we have. Our brains are *quick*.

But sometimes hockey is quicker. At least it is quicker than *my* brain. There are times on the ice when the whizzing of things outwits my here-you-are and makes my body go blank. For some period of time—who knows how long? I don't; I'm blank—I am lost in the rush of things. Then suddenly I come awake to find myself moving fast with a stick in my hand, sometimes a stick I seem to be manipulating with a mysterious purpose. This awakening is always a shock. For a few moments, not only do I not know where I am—I don't even know that I am a human being. Looking down at my stick, I can accept that those huge, bizarre, black leather gloves are my actual hands, and that the slippery way my feet move is the normal way creatures like me get around.

Lately, as we skate and scrimmage, I find that these blankouts are happening less and less. Now I seem to feel my way through the treachery of the forest, not easily, not necessarily at top speed, but with a here-you-are that is starting to figure this whiz-zip game out.

It really is *feeling* my way. At first I tried to think, to calculate in my head whether or not I could cut ahead of this guy and scoot behind that one without running into that third one. But you can't think your way through it; taking long enough to consider like that will leave you spun around and knocked down every time. Instead, you have to simply turn yourself over to your automatic brain. You have to give it a while to learn how hockey works, all on its own. You have to take some falls, a *lot* of falls, you have to mess up your teammates a lot by getting in their way, you have to look stupid and clumsy. But your brain eventually starts to *get it*.

Much the same thing operates when you make plays with the puck, or take a defensive action. But then the automatic part of your brain can call up some help from what you have soaked up, if you have kept your eyes open.

My eyes are always open. There are many skills I lack, but *watching* is not one of them. I am the kind of person who watches and analyzes everything, and as long as I have been watching hockey I have been figuring it out. *Why did that player do what he did? How many options did he have? What could have worked better? What would have failed?* A pro hockey game is like a book. I memorize the book, and keep rereading it in my mind. A kids' hockey game, a good one, is like a rough draft of a book, and if you reread it you can see how it might turn into the real thing with some revising. This is how I spend most of my time when I am alone.

And to my relief I am now finding that all of this mental work *can* pay off. Instead of thinking "Aha, now you are carrying the puck on the forehand against a checker who is also a righthanded shot, so that his forehand sweeps directly against yours, which means that if you slide the puck ahead that way in your natural stickhandling motion it will be like pitching a baseball right to him, whereas if you *start* to do that and then pull it back toward your skates just out of his reach and lift your stick he will swing his forehand through the ice in front of you and be half turned and off-balance and you can kick the puck with your left skate behind him and cut that way and he will be completely out of the picture . . ." I just approach the situation and find myself *doing it.*

What a relief.

The other day, Coach Cooper got me thinking about how this stuff works. I was skating away from the gate despite the signal that we were supposed to get right off. I always do that, even though the Zamboni driver hates it and honks his obnoxious airhorn at me while he waits to get on the ice. Why should I waste two minutes standing on my skates in line, when I could be skating? I always sprint back up the ice and slip into the last place in line just as the kid in front of me is stepping off, so I never really delay anything. When I first started skating last year my dad told me, "Always be the last kid off the ice," and it was just the right thing to say. I get every second of my ice time.

Anyway, I was heading off to the far end to take my last two minutes, and Coach Cooper peeled away from the group and caught up to me. He just skated with me for a while, then he said, "How you feeling about yourself, Woodsie?"

I was pretty tired from practice, so I didn't really

think and plan, I just spoke. "I feel okay. Sometimes I get mad at myself because I'm so slow on open ice. But I'm happy with other stuff that's getting better. And mostly I'm happy to be playing at all."

He nodded. We skated. The Zamboni driver honked. Coach Coop gave a friendly wave as if the guy had just said "Hi!" very cheerfully.

"You're a thinker," he told me. "I can see that. You *see* the ice very well, and you look ahead at where things are going to develop. That's a gift, Woodsie. It's an even better gift than quick feet: One of your thoughts is always going to be faster than anyone else's legs. Even Cody's."

"Maybe. But I'd trade a few thoughts for his crossover."

He laughed, but he stayed serious. "Look. Like most gifts, 'thinking' is hard to figure. You don't know where it came from or how it works, but don't worry about it. Just let it happen. One day, you're going to be our best passer, our best play-maker. Some of these kids already know that."

The horn honked again. Coach ignored it for another half minute, then started us back toward the gate. He veered away to pick up the puck bucket, and I skated off. In the locker room, he showed up as usual to put us through what he calls our "catechism" while we stripped off our pads. We were used to it. But this time I really heard what he meant, and it echoed with his words on the ice and gave me a great thrill.

"What's the fastest way to move the puck?" he hollered.

"*Pass!*" everybody screamed.

"What are the three parts of a pass?"

"*Stop! Look! Pass!*"

"What's the most important part?"

"*Look!*"

He nodded. He paused, and looked around, as he always did. As his eyes passed over me, one of them winked.

"Last question," he said. "What's your most important piece of hockey equipment?"

"*My brain!*" everybody yelled.

Or at least everybody but Cody. He waited until the resonance had died down, and then, with perfect timing, he said in a squeaky voice, "My cup!"

As we laughed, his father looked over at him and shook his head sadly. "That's my son," he said.

"The only kid in the world who would rather pee than think."

He left, and we all started throwing balls of tape.

fifteen

On Friday night my mother comes over to our house, wearing a black baseball cap with the Wings logo on the front. We all greet her enthusiastically, as if she were an aunt coming in from out of town, whom we are glad to see. We *are* glad to see her, and she *is* coming from out of town, pretty much; certainly our shambly old bungalow in Takoma Park has little in common with her Georgetown environment. And after five minutes, she no longer seems like an aunt.

My father makes her a pot of tea, chatting until it is served, then he tactfully disappears. Thea and I talk to mom about school while she drinks her first cup; then she nods to Thea and turns to me, and it is *Thea's* turn to vanish. I sit tight.

"Tomorrow you leave for your hockey games."

"Yes."

"Are you happy?"

"Unbelievably. Thank you for making it possible for me—"

"That's fine," she says, pretending to brush aside my thanks, but obviously pleased with what she sometimes calls her "empowering" role. She reaches into her purse and pulls out a small envelope.

"This should cover your expenses for meals and entertainment," she says. "Also, there is enough here for you to pay your share of the transportation costs—gas and so on."

"Dad already gave Coach Cooper money for that," I say, "and he—"

"Then I shall pay your father back," she says. "This is part of 'hockey' and 'hockey' is my treat." She smiles in a satisfied way that is nevertheless entirely generous. "After all, if it weren't for my insistence, you probably would be playing all your games at that terrible outdoor rink down the road, instead of traveling to distant first-class facilities. Because, remember, it was I who demanded that you pursue the Best."

I nod and start to thank her again. She waves it off. Then she looks me in the eyes for a long moment.

"If you really want to show gratitude," she says quietly, "you could do so by going and putting on your uniform for me."

"Oh, Mom," I groan. "I wish I could. But we don't have them yet. We paid for it and all, but the sweaters haven't come back from the person who sews the numbers and names on. If they don't come tonight we're going to have to play in our practice jerseys—"

She smiles, and holds out a brown paper package. In black marker on the outside is written SQ A WOODS 13.

"Mom!" I take it and rip the paper. Beautiful sky-blue light seems to be flashing from inside, surrounded by luminous snow. My hands tremble a little as they touch smooth, thick cloth. Slowly, letting the heavy sleeves unfold by themselves, I lift first the white home sweater, then the blue road one.

"There are two pairs of socks, too," my mother says.

The sweaters seem huge; they make me feel big enough to wear them. The embroidered flying wing is the size of my head.

"Aren't they a bit oversized?"

"I wear all kinds of pads under them."

"How would I know?" she says with a fake heavy sigh.

I look at her. "Oh, I get what you mean. Sure. I'll go put my junk on."

"Junk!" she says. "Junk doesn't cost three hundred dollars!"

I change fast, putting on everything but my cup and my skates. I choose the road jersey and socks; they match my black hockey pants perfectly. I jump back downstairs.

"Oh, my word," says my mom. Her eyes gape, and through them passes a small flinch.

"I must look big," I say. "Bigger than you expected, I guess."

She shakes her head slowly, widening her eyes. I am amazed to see tears just below the edges. "Oh, Dix. You just look so—" She shrugs, shakes her head again. "So—official. So much like something beyond a small boy who plays."

"I still play," I say, placing my stick on the floor and taking hockey position. "I just play with different toys."

"Oh, cool," comes Thea's voice from behind me. "You got 13. *Very* cool."

She and my father stand at the foot of the stairs. My father is gulping and looking a little lost, just like my mom. They glance at each other.

"Come on," I say. "It's not like I'm going away to college tomorrow. I don't even shave yet."

"It's not that you look so grown up," says Dad. "It's just—" He gulps, smiles tight-lipped at my mom, looks back at me. "It's just—you look so—so—so very much like someone dressed up to be a bruise in a kindergarten play!"

They all bust up. "Those padded pants *are* pretty swollen," my mother hoots.

"The helmet should be that gross yellowish color," jeers Thea, "that bruises start to turn when they, like, heal."

"That's it," I say. "I'm changing." But upstairs in my room, when I take the sweaters off, I lay them out on the bed, one with the logo up, the other with the number. And the name. It says 13. And it says Woods.

"Woods," I say. "Number thirteen, Woods." But it doesn't fit yet. The name on the sweater doesn't feel like mine. I fold everything up, put it neatly back into my hockey bag. There's no reason the name *should* feel right yet. It's a hockey player's name on a hockey player's sweater. Tomorrow, when I take the ice, when the puck is dropped and I go after it, when I get a little sweat and snow on it, from inside and out, then, I know, it will fit just fine.

ava outsticks me in the corner and twists the puck away, back-skating quickly to the top of the circle. Like a sucker I chase for two strides, angry that I lost the puck. But a defenseman isn't supposed to chase the puck up high; a defenseman is supposed to stay low, either in the corner, in front of the net, or behind it; I am out of position and Java knows it. He grins, and fakes a shot. I lunge; out of the corner of my eye I see both Dooby and Zip slide over to face the shot.

But Java stops short of slapping the puck, and instead whips it through the slot to Cody near the face-off dot in the left circle.

Dooby dives at the puck, but it skips over his stick, leaving him on his belly out of the play.

Zip sees Cody take the pass, and skates sharply toward him, challenging him *way* out there in the circle, hoping Cody will one-time a shot to be smothered. But Cody just has time to skate back one stride and pull the puck way around to his forehand. Falling backwards, he peers around the blocky shape of Zip rushing at him and slings a beauty of a shot, soft and straight, just what he had to do. Zip crashes into him. The net is open. We all watch in horror as the puck cruises in its perfect path.

Or, rather, *almost* all of us watch. Trusty Woodsie the Defender (ta-*dah*!), just a moment ago so desperately out of position, has somehow foreseen just this situation, and here he is, coolly skating through the crease, smoothly taking the puck on his forehand two inches from the goal line, continuing through the circle, flipping the puck off the boards as he jumps over the tangle of Zip and Cody, picking it up on the other side of them, faking toward the boards by leaning his shoulders as Barry skates over to intercept him, then cutting back to the center and going by. Over the blue line, over the red line, head down, pushing the puck up ahead. Hearing *ssschwunch ssschwunch* behind him as the bad guys chase. Crossing the other blue line, hitting the top of the circle, looking up, keeping the feet moving.

Here we are once more at that little gap between the rush and the celebration.

This time, though, Woodsie the Breakaway Dynamo doesn't hesitate to think. He puts the puck out on his forehand and leans that way, dipping his right shoulder to loft the shot. The goalie slides over, drops to his knees, glove up, blocker down.

Woodsie yanks the puck back through the crease, half turns as he passes the post, and flicks it backhanded with the tip of his stick blade.

From behind the cage, through the white net, he watches the puck slide in and kick around the goal.

A cry goes up from center ice. "Oh no, not another defenseman who rushes the puck!"

"Bobby Orr, guys!"

"Hoo, got a Brian Leetch wanna-be!"

"Stay at home, defense, stay at home!"

The four guys on my shift wham into me, knocking me back against the boards. I barely keep my skates down as I get bumped around. "He *shoots*," screams Dooby, "he gets incredibly *lucky*, he *scores*!"

"And tonight," hollers Cody, who has caught up and joined the crowd, "we get to paint his buns with hot mustard from the snack bar, to celebrate his first goal!" (I already know this is a fake threat; they worried another rookie named Jack for half a practice after he poked in a rebound two weeks ago.)

As we skate away the goalie, our back-up, name of Marshall, glares at me out of his mask. "It's just a scrimmage, chump," he says. "Let's see you do it in a real game."

"Against a real goalie, you mean?"

He laughs. "Talk to me Saturday night, Mario. If you can stop sniffling. You're raw, chump. They like raw meat up in Philly. You're going to have teeth marks all over you."

Tomorrow I guess we'll see.

Playing

The feeling in the locker room surprises me. I'm not sure what I expected. Leading up to our first game, my feelings have been swooping back and forth between an almost silly excitement and grim seriousness. In the van coming up, Cody was incredibly goofy, turning everything into a joke, while his dad was willing at any time to talk calmly about hockey strategy and mechanics. But once we found the rink, lugged our bags and sticks inside, located our locker room, welcomed the other kids as they drifted in, the two extremes of feeling went away and we all seemed to be left in the middle: pretty happy, pretty focused, pretty relaxed.

It is the relaxation that I didn't anticipate. I think it comes mostly from the veterans—Barry, which you'd kind of expect, and Dooby and Zip and Cody, which you wouldn't. But here, getting ready for the game, it's as if these guys are a couple of years older all of a sudden—more "mature" as my mother would say. Serious, but easy about it. No fakey let's-get-mean scowling snarling act.

For the first time I get the idea that maybe good athletes prepare to play by finding the part of their nature that is calm, confident, even patient. I always thought athletes must feel scared and nervous *or* braggy and cocky and "pumped." You watch a football game and you see the players crashing into each other and hollering *"Yaaaah!"* into each other's faces and shaking their fists at everyone, and you think, "Well, I guess you've got to get *up* to play." You watch a baseball game and you see the guys sitting around frowning in concentration as if they were about to take a three-hour standardized math test, and you think, "Well, I guess you've got to get *down* to play."

But the Wings just seem to be cool. It's a relief to me. It feels good to blend into the coolness. Frankly I was worried about how I might have to act. If I had to scream *"Yaaah!"* into anyone's face I would feel unbelievably stupid. If I had to frown and pretend I wasn't about to have fun, I'd feel really false.

Instead, I get to just sit and smile mildly and

watch and listen. Boot notices my expression and says, "Looks like Woodsie got into the Ritalin. There'll be no hitting in front of the net on *his* shifts."

"It's beautiful, man," I say, with my eyes half-lidded. "Everything is beautiful. All of my, like, fellow humans are welcome to share my space."

"Yeah, dude," says Cody, imitating my mellow tone. "We're, like, all really brothers, man. Why can't we all just be, you know, like, *nice*? Why can't we have peace on the mother planet? Let's, like, start the peace, man, out there today, with these wonderful Pennsylvanians."

"That would be cool, Codes."

"Yeah. We'll start today."

"Right after, like, the third period."

"Yeah. Just as soon as we finish completely, like, kicking their heads in."

"It will be so nice to shake their hands in brotherhood, after we have broken a few of their arms and things, man."

"There was once a game in Maple Leaf Gardens in which four players suffered broken arms, three left and one right—"

"Thank you, Shinny. That was mellow."

Coach Cooper isn't in the locker room for most of the time. He comes in once with a roster sheet we all have to sign next to our name, birth date, and uniform number. He comes in again with a bucket of pucks that he leaves by the door. Then he finally comes in to stay, about ten minutes before game time.

Everyone looks at him and gets quiet, even Cody.

"Okay," Coach says. I notice that he has wet and combed his hair, which is very thick and usually stands out all over his head. He has also put on a white turtleneck, a blue pullover parka with a small Wings logo over the heart, and some khaki pants with a crease in them instead of his usual jeans.

I am not the only one to notice. Just as Coach starts to speak again, Dooby says, "You look real nice, Coach."

"Yes, you do," says Zip.

"Thanks," says Coach. "Now, these—"

"I'd even say *cute*, wouldn't you, Zip?"

"Well, Doobs, I don't know about *THAT*. I think 'lovely' is a better—"

Coach holds up his hand. The boys stop. Coach waits for a few seconds.

"Okay," he says again. "Did any of you look at their side of the roster you signed?"

I raise my hand.

"What did you see, Woodsie?"

"They're all pretty old," I say.

He nods. "Very good. That's right. These guys are on the very edge of the age line. Some of them turn twelve this month. Which means what?"

Boot raises his hand. Coach points to him. "It means they're beginning to struggle with the conflicting impulses inspired by perfectly natural hormonal awakenings," he says.

Coach rolls his eyes. "What else?"

"It means they are also probably huge."

"And they have that gritty-looking stubble on their cheeks."

"And other subtle changes in the physiology."

"Okay," says Coach. "I have just been in their locker room. And they *are* huge. A couple of them probably weigh close to one hundred fifty pounds. How much do you weigh, Princey?"

"In pounds or kilograms?"

"Pounds, please."

"I weigh seventy-one pounds."

"Thank you. So are we going to go out and try to outmuscle them at the blue line when we carry the puck into their zone?"

"You bet," says Zip, who of course will not be carrying anything across any blue lines. "We're not afraid of anything, right, hombres?"

"What we'll do," says Coach, "is dump to the corners and cut around them and beat them to the puck. I'll be surprised if they are as quick as we are."

Dooby raises his hand. "Except for Woodsie and Mike, sir. The two of them are *terribly* pokey."

"Thank you for the clarification, Doober, and for that kindly team spirit we all count on from you. So I want the strong side winger and the center to chase the puck, the off-wing to head for the low slot, and *one* defenseman to creep in toward the top of the circle and watch. If one of us gets the puck and the slot is covered, pass it back quickly to the defenseman and head for the net as he takes a quick shot." He turns to where the defensemen are sitting as a group, and points at us. "I want *low shots*," he says. "Don't try to be Mario Lemieux out there, picking the high corners. Just swat it hard and low to the ice and *get it on net*. Okay?"

We nod.

"Another thing. If they plant their biggest guys in front of the cage in our end, don't get caught on their backs, pushing and shoving them from behind. That won't do anything. They won't even feel it. We're going to have to front them, keep them just off your shoulder, intercept the centering passes. But keep peeking to make sure they haven't slipped high or low on you."

He looks around at everyone. "When we have the puck I want you to *look*, and to *pass*. Cody and Prince and Boot and Java and Billy, you're all good stickhandlers, but don't fall in love with yourselves out there today. Pass the puck. Pass it. If we're going to beat these guys with quickness we have to move the puck the fastest way we can."

The door opens and a man with a Flyers cap sticks his head in. "Zam's making the last turn, Coach."

"Thanks." The man goes. Coach looks at a sheet of paper. "Here are the lines: Billy centering Java and Mike. Shinny centering Mason and

Marshall. Prince centering Cody and Boot. That line will start. Now, defense pairs: Doober with Barry. Woodsie with Jake. Ernie with Feets. Jake and Woodsie start."

For a moment I am disappointed; I had hoped to be paired with either Dooby or Barry, both of whom are completely dependable and alert. Defensemen have to communicate a lot on the ice—*who's got that man? Who's going to the corner after the puck and who's staying home in the slot? Who's pinching in to punch the puck back in deep, and who's tearing down the ice early to cover the rush?* I wanted to work with someone safe. But Jake, another new Wing like me, is a total airhead. He has good skills, but he doesn't pay attention from one ten-second segment to the next. But then I realize: maybe that's why coach has paired him with me. Because he's counting on *me* to be the Dooby or Barry of my group. Because, I am, you know, such a great thinker and all.

"I'll take the biggest guy," Jake says with a mean growl, slugging me hard on the shoulder.

"I don't think that's a good way to divide the assignments, Jake."

"Whatever," he says, punching the wall.

Coach Cooper lines us up at the door, behind Zip, who is quiet now. Coach looks up the line with his hand on the door handle. "This is going to be a good season," he says. I can hear my blood booming around my body as if it's looking for an open window to get a little air. Maybe I have never been this excited. "Let's give it a good start. Look. Think. Play hard. Have fun."

He opens the door.

"Let's roll, *Wings!*" hollers Barry. Others mumble and roar. We teeter across the rubber floor to the open corner-gate like seals at the zoo belly-flopping excitedly over the ground to the cool, blue pool—and then at last we are where *we* belong, where *we* can move smooth and fast, where *we* can do tricks: the ice.

The warmups start, then they are over; I never really focus on anything that is happening but I suppose I skate and shoot as directed. We gather at the bench for a few rah-rah words I don't really hear. Then the others sit down, and six of us skate out.

Zip heads toward the net. I skate fast to catch

up, so I can tap his left leg pad and say, "Be tough, Zipper!" or something idiotic like that. But before I can speak he looks at me and snaps, "Get out of my face you incredible nerd."

"Sorry," I say.

"Just keep those jerks from screening me, duck-butt." He skates to his crease, and I go line up behind my forwards.

For the first time, I think to look at the members of the Longview Lightning, our opponents. They wear white jerseys with orange-and-black trim. They are indeed very big. My first feeling about them is a gush of hockey brotherhood (as Cody joked). But then all of a sudden—I can't say why—I decide I hate them to their sorry hulking bones.

The puck is dropped. The Lightning center pulls it back to his left defenseman, who skates three strides and fires it hard down the left boards.

Time to skate.

"I got the puck," I yell to Jake, who glances at me blankly and gets blindsided by their right wing. I turn and tear toward the cage. I have two steps on the center and one on the left wing. Zip has come out of the net to stop the hard-around with his stick; he leaves it for me and slips back around to the front of the net.

I hear the forwards bearing down from behind as I get to the puck, and at the last second I see that the other wing has somehow gotten to the right post. I fight a flash of panic—*I thought they were slow*—and neatly yank the puck past my skates without stopping, to the corner, where Prince ought to be waiting. Unfortunately, doing this stands me up straight with my arms tucked back and along the boards, still moving forward fast. The right wing steps out from the post and simply lets me hit him. My skates fly out. I smack flat onto my back, helmet chunking into the ice a half second later. The lights way up in the rafters seem to dive at me and then recede as if they were on bungee cords.

I hear a few shouts. I remember that I should get up. I wriggle and turn toward the wall and realize I don't have my stick, and I look over my left shoulder for it. Instead of my stick I see Zip on his back, and the referee bending past him to get the puck out of the net.

"Change!" I hear Coach Cooper's voice from far away. I must get up, get off. Where's my stick?

"Didn't see that one, did you?" says Zip. He sounds chipper, but he's furious. I shake my head.

"Left wing cut to the corner, you passed it to him perfectly, he slapped it through Cody's skates, Jake was still on his back and you were too by now, their center takes it and jams it between my pads. Now get off the ice."

"Good shift," says the Lightning right wing as I skate for the bench. Then he hands me my stick.

Sitting down, trying to clear my head, I tell myself it's okay, no problem, anyone can get messed up on his very first shift, next one will be better, we'll get the goal back. I hear a whistle and look down the ice. Zip is on his face in the crease, Shinny is on his butt in the left circle, three Lightning players are hugging in the slot.

"Change," says the coach.

I try to focus, to watch, to get my here-you-are warmed up. But this is different from what I have been watching and playing for the past few weeks. I cannot even keep up with the puck with my *eyes*. I see it dart between two players, I see white jerseys weaving and crossing, I see a flicker of black on the ice, more weaving, I watch the side of the ice I saw it fly into, but then on the other side I hear a *thwot* and look over in time to see six arms raised. Score! Where did the puck go during that time?

"Change."

My turn. Face-off. Their center, instead of pulling the puck back, chips it forward right at me and shoulders his way past Cody, who falls. I look down at it coming neatly toward my stick blade, and glance up at the last second just to check on that center. To my surprise he leaps my stick and hurtles past me without paying any attention. But I'm the one with the puck! I look down to line it up on the heel of my stick for a pass up the boards.

It isn't there. Behind me there are shouts, a whistle, hoots. I don't even turn. Why bother? I am still in position for the face-off. The puck must have hopped my stick and kept moving nicely into the zone behind me, where the center picked it up for a breakaway and scored.

It was too fast for Coach even to count it as a shift. We lose the next face-off, their right defenseman dumps, I skate back, beat a winger to it, hesitate for a second deciding what to do, and someone behind me reaches a stick between my skates and taps the puck to the winger facing me. He tries to stuff it in the short side but it bounces off the post into the crease.

I turn. The center, who was behind me, is on his way for the easy goal. I lunge at him with my stick, hook his upper arm, and fall into the back of the net. He goes down too. Whistle. Penalty. Woodsie to the box.

"Change."

At the end of the first period the score is 8–0.

Shots on goal: 21 for the Lightning, none for the Wings.

Penalty minutes: 12 for the Wings (all well-deserved), 2 for the Lightning.

Minutes my shift has been on the ice: About 5. Of those, minutes I have been on my butt or my back: a good 4.

The Lightning pump in two goals on the first shift of the second period, then add another one minute later. Skating off, I look at the scoreboard. It still reads 8–0.

The scorekeeper is saving our feelings by not

putting the mounting lead up for all to see. Of course, we know he is doing that—so does everyone in the stands—and that makes it all the more humiliating. Hockey players don't want charity. I'd rather see the 13 or 16 or 20 to nothing. I'd rather face it.

But in fact I lose count of the goals. Then, midway through the third period, for a moment I can't remember if this is our second game of the day or our first. It sure *feels* like our second, but—no, that's right, this is the first one, it was morning when we entered this rink. I remember lining up so excited in the locker room.

I remember thinking Cody and Prince were fast.

I remember thinking Barry and Dooby were the toughest, craftiest defensemen possible. And Zip was an awesome goalie.

I watch blankly as the Lightning players wheel around in big curves and make long passes to each other to kill the time. (At one point I heard their coach holler, "Four passes before a shot, four passes!" meaning he wanted them to delay their shots on us until they had dallied through four exchanges. More charity.) I face the fact: *This* is hockey. What these big fast clever tough talented Pennsylvania boys are playing is the sport I *thought* I was ready to play. But I am not even close. I cannot even follow it from the bench. When I am on, supposedly *playing*, I am helpless. The game is happening around me. Around *us*.

The only one who seems to keep up with it all is Coach Cooper. Through the whole thing he is calm and genial, almost mild. The words of advice he speaks to the players are precise. He never hollers like the other coach does. He never sounds anything but attentive. You'd swear the score was 2–2. He just seems to be *talking* to you, and you hear him clearly. Backing up on a charging winger with the puck, I had no idea what to do, and I heard him saying, "Poke, poke," so I poked, and the puck popped off the kid's stick and Cody backhanded it to center ice. It worked! A defensive play! I smiled inside my helmet, pumped a fist.

I wonder what Coach is thinking and feeling as the game winds down. How will he spin this in the locker room? *"Good effort, boys!"*? *"Some bad breaks at the beginning, and we just could never pick it up!"*? *"They're an experienced group, guys—we'll get there!"*?

Is he as crushed as we are? Is he ashamed of us? Is he ashamed of himself, for not warning us?

But what could he have said, as a warning? *"By the way, keep in mind that you fellows reek. Don't go out there with any hopes of even getting in their way. Just let the waves wash over you, and always wear a smile."*

The horn sounds. I look at the scoreboard. Shots: 58 to 6. Final score (they flash it up now, just for the record): 21 to 1. I was vaguely aware that somewhere near the end of the third period Shinny got a long wobbly shot under the goalie's blocker arm. No one even cheered. Coach Cooper waited until Shinny came off at the end of the shift, and tapped him on the helmet without a word.

We totter back into the locker room. It is a lot farther than it was coming out. We go through the door. We sit. We strip off our helmets and drop them. No one moves to take off his skates.

"Well," says Prince, *"That* was sort of cool. I mean, I've never actually died before."

No one laughs or argues. Prince shuts up.

"Shinny," says the Coach as he comes in the

door with our second sticks. "Shinner, don't even think about telling me when the last time was in hockey history that a team got beat 21–1." He dumps our sticks into the corner with a small crash. They all stay standing.

"It was last year," says Dooby, leaning back against the wall with his eyes closed.

Coach Cooper looks at him. "What?"

"It was last year. Last season. The last time a team got beat this bad." He opens his bright eyes briefly to look over at Barry. "It was us did the beating. We beat Doverville 22–2 and Bingham 20–0. The Squirt A Wings, I mean."

Things get even quieter. "Yeah, well," says Coach Coop, pulling off one skate. "You know what they say. 'That was then, and—'"

"'And that was *hockey*,'" says Boot.

"Was it, Norman?" says Zip. He is looking out from under lowered eyelids, leaning against the wall, seemingly held up only by his stiff pads. His face is pale. If a face can look limp, his does. But the eyes are not limp—they're furious! "Then why not go join them and play some '*hockey*' again?"

There is a crackling silence. Finally Boot looks at

Barry, then around the room. He is more angry than ashamed.

"Don't get on me," he says. "I stayed here, didn't I?"

"Then *stay* here, Boot, and don't whine about it," says Dooby. "We all stayed for reasons that don't get wiped out by losing bad."

Boot says quietly, "I didn't think it would be *this* bad."

"Neither did those teams we killed last year," says Cody.

Boot looks at him. "But *you* know what I mean, Codes. It's just, you know, once you've played like *that*—"

"Right," says Barry. "Once you've been a big-time winner you forget it's hard. We did—we forgot. We were all kind of tagging along with Peter and Jason and Kenny, with his eighty goals. We didn't even think we were holding them back. We thought we were playing *with* them." He unwraps tape from his right sock and drops it, not bothering to ball it up. He shakes his head. Barry has never said this much since I've known him, and he's uncomfortable. "Like I said, it's hard. You got to love hockey."

"I love hockey as much as you do," snaps Boot.

Zip, still unmoving, says, "Well, good for you, Boot. Way to be. Hey—I played with you in your first game, with the Mite B's. You scored two goals. You skated around all dipsy-doo and nobody touched you. Of *course* you love hockey!"

Barry points at me. I look down quickly. "What about Woodsie over here, Boot? This was *his* first game. Think he's in love yet? I sure don't hear him whining."

Everyone pulls tape for a few moments. I can feel my scalp hot and red beneath my soaking hair, and I won't look up. Then Boot says, "Well, anyway, Woodsie's the reason we *lost* this game."

Heads snap in his direction. I look too. He shakes his head at me in disgust. "Yeah," he says, "if he could have been just a *little* sharper running that defensive zone two-man trap Coach gave us . . ."

"That's right," says Cody. "And I thought his decision-making during the neutral-zone pick-and-weave play *really* sucked."

"What about those backhand drop passes in the high slot?" says Dooby, shaking his head sadly. "They were *pret-ty* wobbly."

"Wobbly backhand drop passes in the high slot are certainly the reason *I* didn't score," says Prince.

"Me, too."

"Yeah, Woodsie, thanks a *lot*."

"Suck some *more*, Woodsie."

"Have some *skills*, Woodsie."

I try to tell myself it's funny. It's funny, sure. And of course I like being accepted enough to get abused. I try to smile. But the fact is, I cannot. I cannot speak, either. Because I am angry. I have just discovered that I am one of those jerks who hates to lose so bad that maybe he can't get over it.

We continue to dress, not as quietly as a little while ago. A few minutes later, somebody throws a tape ball. Somebody throws it back. Somebody cusses, somebody laughs. Three people talk, then six. Then you can't tell how many.

When the jabber has reached almost its usual level, Cody pops up, slings his bag on his shoulder, and heads for the door. He is always the first one out of uniform, and he always leaves the room without saying anything in the way of good-bye.

But today he pauses by the door and turns to

face the room. One by one we all notice, and the talk stops. He waits until it's quiet again, and he has every eye on him.

"Well," he says, sounding more serious than I have ever heard him, "I just want to remind you. I mean, speaking for myself, I have something to prove this afternoon." He looks around. "You guys, you *Wings*, know what I'm saying?"

There is an awkward silence; it looks like a few guys are trying to think seriously again. Jake stands up, fire in his eye. "Cody's right," he says, raising his fist. "We got to show we're tough, we won't give in, we—"

"Oh shut up you incredible dweeb," says Cody. He rolls his eyes. "I'm *talking* about my donut record."

"What?" says Jake.

"Last year, after our first game, I singlehandedly consumed seven strawberry custard donuts in five minutes."

"*With* sprinkles," says Dooby.

"*Without* puking," adds Zip.

Cody nods. "Thank you. And about fifteen minutes from now, at the counter of a donut shop

I noticed down the road on the way here, surrounded by doubters and supporters alike, I plan to prove that last year was no fluke. Be there," he says, with a last challenging look around, "if you have *any* sense of tradition." He walks out.

And twenty minutes later, with fifteen hockey players crowding around him shouting repulsive ideas about what strawberry custard might *really* be, Cody, the Coach's son, the leader, eats eight.

On the edge of the crowd, I try to laugh with them. Nope. I try just to smile. No. Amusement stands far away from me, a stranger without access, not wearing ice skates. I face it: I am still hurt, still mad, still feeling the hockey, the humiliation. The game is over. These guys are having fun; what is wrong with me?

A voice comes quietly from behind my left shoulder.

"If this clowning crap strikes you as stupid, don't worry," says Zip.

I turn and look back at him. He is watching Cody, eyes still half-lidded. He flicks a look at me, then goes back to the laughers.

"You know, don't you?" he says. I can see that

he too is still furious. "You know. That's why you can't laugh. You know," he says, turning and heading for the door, "that it ain't about *donuts*. It ain't about *fun*. It's about hockey! And hockey's enough."

Here's a sneak peek at the next book in the
Wolfbay Wings ice hockey
series by Bruce Brooks

available from HarperCollins

I'm reading one of my brother's big-deal collectible Sandman books and bending back the cover because I am a mean little jerk when I hear Kenny Moseby holler up for me from the yard. Moseby used to come to the front door and knock, being a very polite boy, but one time my mother answered the door, told him she would get me, and on her way to get me heard something blow up in the kitchen, which she went to fix in kind of a panic. She forgot about leaving Moze on the doormat. It is typical of Moze that he just stood there waiting, wouldn't knock again, for almost half an hour. Since then he comes around beneath my window and hollers, "Hey, Zip."

Used to be six or seven times a day. But he hasn't been around for about a month now.

I don't bother to get up. "Get poked," I yell, hoping I sound bored.

"Hey, Zip," he repeats, as if he hadn't just said it.

"Get reamed."

"Hey, Zip."

"Get tooled."

And so on. Finally I run out of verbs. Verbs are the only words I like; I have a lot of them. I go to the window and look down.

Moseby's standing there flat-footed, hands at his sides, looking up flat-faced. I open the window and spit, making sure I miss, but not by much.

"Sorry, Moze," I say. "I have a puck in my throat and it makes me kind of hawk a lot. I'll probably have it surgically removed after the season if it doesn't get dislodged by another one between now and then."

He swallows, and says, "I heard it was bad."

"It wasn't *bad*," I say. "And I heard you had four goals in two games and six assists in another."

He kind of nods, looking away from my eyes.

"Now *that's* bad," I say. "*That* sucks."

"Listen, Zip—"

"In fact, I think *you* suck, Moze, so good-bye." I try to slam the window down, but wooden windows don't really slam in late October.

I go back to the graphic novel and bend the cover worse. Too bad for my brother. It isn't *his* fault my best friend left my hockey club and went off and scored like 41 goals in three games for the enemy while my team lost three games by a margin of like 236 goals, all but 17 scored on me. I guess there is no justice.

A minute later Moseby walks into my room.

"I just opened the door," he explains, very guilty.

"That's what one does with doors," I say. "Congratulations." I keep reading.

He sprawls on Scott's bed. Nobody says dip. Then he kind of casually says, "So, how does Scott like Bantams?"

"He says they will never lose which means he will never play, so Bantams are unpleasant too in their own special way. But not of course like Squirts. And not like me. I *play*."

"I'm sorry you got hammered," he says.

"No problem, Mozer."

He nods as if he believes me. Which of course makes me madder, so after another minute I throw the book across the room. The spine hits the wall hard, just below Scott's Joe Juneau poster; the sharp noise sounds a little like a puck snapping onto a stick blade, and that makes Moseby's antennae twitch. His mouth's probably watering too. Moseby's entire mind and body drops everything at any stimulus that suggests hockey action.

I used to really like this about him—in fact, I was in awe of it though most of the time I mocked him. It was one of the reasons we were pals. I like hockey all right, but I am not in love with it. I never hustle in practice, I gripe about skating drills, I goof off, I never concentrate except during games. When I don't hustle, people accept it because I am a goalie and taking it slack is a goalie thing. But it's just that I don't give a puck sometimes. Every week or so I think about quitting, and the idea never really hurts. I keep playing, but usually not by much of a margin. It's just easier to play than to stop. My dad would flip. Since I started playing hockey he has become a vice president of the Wolfbay club, and he is one of the co-managers of the rink, and my mom's friends are all hockey moms now, and it's a complete family lifestyle. It wasn't that way when Scott was the only one playing. They thought

Scott was just weird to take up this bizarre ice game. When the Baby started, it became a family deal. Now they all like it a lot more than I do.

Moseby is not like me. Moseby cannot remember his childhood before he started skating at age five. He doesn't care about those years—who needs to remember a time when you liked fire trucks? Life started with hockey. Listen, Moze doesn't sleep but about three hours a night. He lies there twitching with the awful feeling that, somewhere, someone is skating with a puck *without him*, and this drives him nuts. Moseby will quit hockey when the undertaker peels his cold, dead fingers from his stick. Once when he had the flu, he thought he was going to die and he called me to issue his final request: He wanted to be buried in his skates *without the blade guards* and he wanted to make certain he was dressed in his *road* uniform, because he always liked it better.

Of course he is the greatest player there is. Not just around here, either—last year he kicked the butts of all the teams from Boston, Minnesota, wherever. Everything from his skating to his shot shows he lives for this, everything shows he has found his joy in life. I think it's sick, but what the heck, maybe I'd be the same if I were that good. I think about that a lot: Is Moze great because he loves it so much, or does he love it so much because he's so good? Because when you're as good as he is, there's more to it than practice. When you're that good, it's because of some extra, weird thing inside.

Since he left the Wings, I hate all this hockey-love stuff in him. All of it strikes me as sick for sure. I wish he'd wake up one day and realize he only cared about girls or chess or some other crap. He sucks.

"So what are you doing here?" I ask, as the Sandman book slides down the wall. "Couldn't resist rubbing it in?"

He turns red, and I feel a little bad for saying something I know isn't even possibly true but which I also know he would treat like it could be. "No, man, jeez, I—"

"What number are you this year, Moze? Still 22?"

He looks puzzled. "I wasn't 22 on the Wings. I was 28. And I'm still 28."

I yawn. "Thought it was 22. Never mind."

That gets him. He turns white. I yawn again. Across the room he droops his head into his hands. I smile.

If I was going to get beat 22–4 on the Wings, and Moze was going to get six goals in a 14–1 victory for Montrose, then he could stand some pain. And I could give it to him.

I smile for a long time.